characters created by
lauren child

We completely must GO to LONDON

PUFFIN

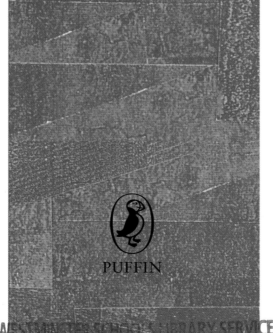

Illustrations from the
TV animation produced
by Tiger Aspect

PUFFIN BOOKS
Published by the Penguin Group: London, New York, Australia,
Canada, India, Ireland, New Zealand and South Africa
Penguin Books Ltd, Registered Offices: 80 Strand, London WC2R ORL, England

puffinbooks.com

First published 2012
Reissued 2014
004

I have this little sister Lola.
She is small and very funny.
Today me and Lola are very excited
because we're going on a school trip to London.

"Have you got everything ready for the trip, Lola?"
I say.

"Yes, Charlie,
I completely must take some...
pink milk

and a
packed lunch

and some **money**

and my **clicky camera.**

And I absolutely have to take **foxy.**

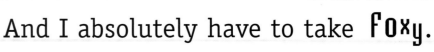

Foxy's got lots of friends
    in **London**, Charlie."

When we get to **London**, Mrs Hanson says
we all have to walk in pairs and stay together
so we don't get **lost**.

I say,
"You must stay with me and Marv, Lola.
London is very big."

"I know, Charlie,
London is extremely HUGE," says Lola.

"And it's completely NOISY,"
says Lotta.

Bing bong!

"That's **Big Ben** chiming,"
I say.

Lola says,
"**Big Ben** makes a very strange sound.
What is the matter with him?"

"Big Ben is the name of the **bell**
inside the **clock**, Lola!"

"I didn't know bells had names, Charlie."

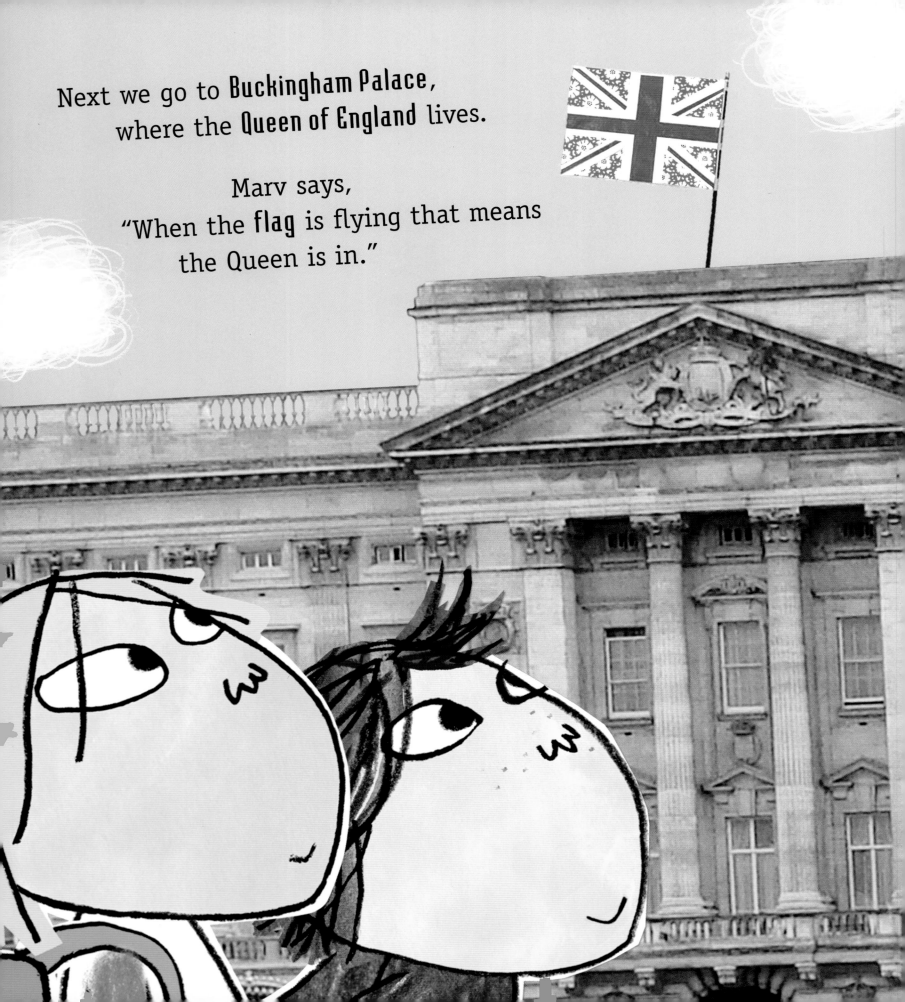

Next we go to Buckingham Palace, where the Queen of England lives.

Marv says, "When the **flag** is flying that means the Queen is in."

"I wonder which window
is the Queen's bedroom,"
says Lola.

"I'm not sure, Lola.
The guidebook says that
there are 52 bedrooms."

Lola says,
"Does she keep her Crowns
and her jewellery
in her bedroom?"

"No, the Queen's most
precious jewels are kept
in the Tower of London.

Mrs Hanson says
we're going to have a look
at them next."

When we get to the **Tower of London**, Lola says,
"What a sparkly crown. Why doesn't the Queen
keep it at home and then she could wear it all the time!"

I say,
"Kings and queens have always kept their jewels
in the tower because it is a very safe place."

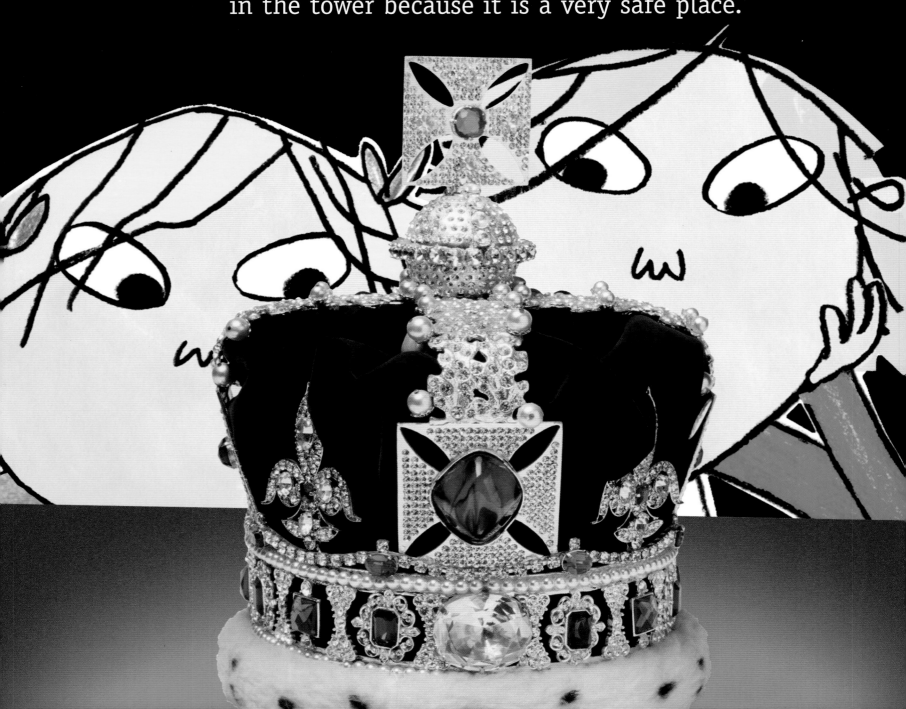

Lola says, "I wonder what olden-day **kings** and **queens** actually looked like."

NATIONAL PORTRAIT GALLERY

"We can see pictures of them here at the National Portrait Gallery."

Lola says,
"I wonder what it would be like
to be a **royal** person, Lotta."

"Yes, yes, yes!" says Lotta.
"We would sit on **thrones**!"

"Me and Charlie would be great **kings**," says Marv. "We could live in huge **castles** and ride horses all day!"

We walk out of the gallery
into Trafalgar Square.

"That is a very high-up statue, Charlie,"
says Lola.

"That is Nelson's Column.
Nelson was a famous admiral in the navy
and he sailed all over the world.
He won the Battle of Trafalgar in 1805."

Lola says,
"I like Sailing, Charlie."

"That's lucky because we're taking a riverboat to a place called Greenwich."

"I like this river," says Lola.
"What's it called?"

"It's called the Thames," says Marv,
"and it goes right through the middle of London.
In the past, people used riverboats
to move things across the city.
There were no lorries then,
so even bread and milk went on the boats."

Lola says,
"What about **pink milk**, Charlie?"

I say,
"I'm not sure they drank **pink milk**
in the olden days, Lola."

When we get to **Greenwich**, Marv says,
"Can we look in the **Royal Observatory**?
I've heard it's famous."

"Yes, but what is an **Ob-ser-va-tory**?"
says Lola.

"It's where people look into **space**.

They see everything through a giant **telescope**," I say.

"And this is the **planetarium**,"
says Marv. "It shows all the **stars** and
planets that are in the night sky."

Lola says,
"We should visit the **moon**, Lotta."

"Yes!" says Lotta.
"We could go there on holiday."

I say,
"Come on, Lola.
It's time to see the **dinosaurs**."

The dinosaur bones are kept
at the **Natural History Museum**.

Me and Marv can't wait.

I say, "Marv, did you know
the **Stegosaurus** had
armour plates on its back?"

Marv says, "And, Charlie,
did you know that the
Diplodocus was as long
as TWO buses put together?"

"Quick, Marv! The **Tyrannosaurus rex** is coming!"
I say.

"Oh no!" says Marv. "Let's escape on the
Pterodactyl's back!"

"He'll NEVER catch us now!"
I say.

"Rrraaaahhhh!"

Suddenly me and Marv
look round, and we can't see
Lola or Lotta anywhere.

"Lola!"

"Lotta!"

"Oh no, where have they gone?"
says Marv.

And I say,
"I don't know!"

We look and look. And at last
we find them... in the gift shop.

I say, "Oh, there you are, Lola.
You weren't meant to wander off."

Lola says, "But we didn't wander off.
We were with Mrs Hanson the
whole time. I think maybe you
and Marv got lost."

"Oh," I say.
"I think we did!"

"Look! We've bought **postcards**," says Lotta.

The last thing we do is go to Lola's most FAVOURITE place of all...

"This is the BIGGEST
      and most best wheel.
It's called the **London Eye**
      because you can see every
single thing when you're up there,"
      says Lola.

"Yes, yes, yes!" says Lotta.
"I can see completely everywhere from up here.
Every single place we have EVER been to."

"And I can see even more THINGS to visit," says Lola.
"We absolutely must come back to London EXTREMELY soon!"

MAP of London

Charlie and Lola have visited all these **places**...
Can you put a **tick** next to the
places YOU have been to?

☐ Natural History Museum

Trafalgar Square (Nelson's Column)

☐ Buckingham Palace

The Houses of Parliament (Big Ben)

☐ The London Eye

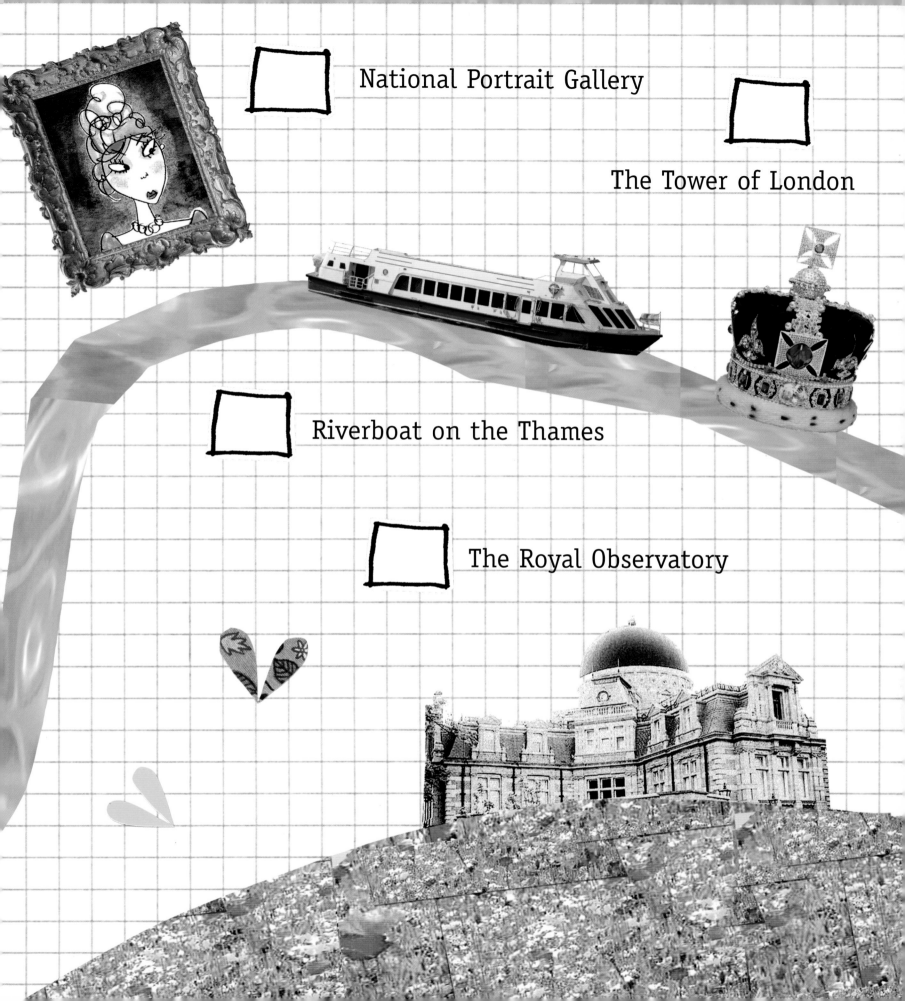

National Portrait Gallery

The Tower of London

Riverboat on the Thames

The Royal Observatory